This book belongs to

....

....

....

First Published 2017 by Ballynafagh Press.
This edition published 2019 by Johnny Magory Business.
Ballynafagh, Prosperous, Naas, Co. Kildare, Ireland

ISBN: 978-0-9935792-5-7

Text, Illustrations, Design © 2019 Emma-Jane Leeson
www.JohnnyMagory.com

Edited, Illustrated and Printed entirely in Ireland.
Proud Partners of CMRF Crumlin. €1 from the sale of this book will be donated to this charity.

Please visit **www.CMRF.org** for more information.

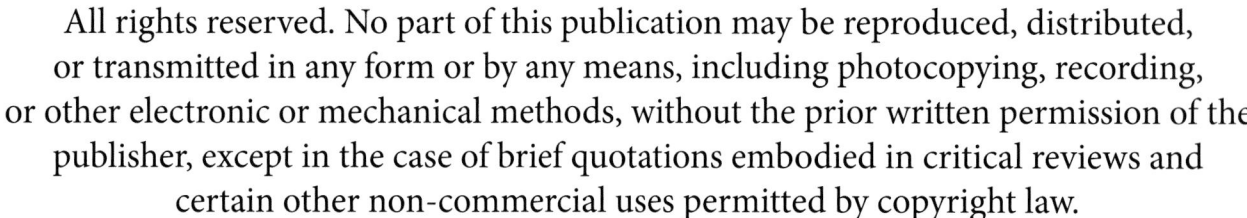

**The Children's Medical
& Research Foundation**
Our Lady's Children's
Hospital, Crumlin

and the Wild Water Race

Emma-Jane Leeson

For Lily-Marie, Eibhean & Layla...
My endless source of imagination fuel!

I'll tell you a story about Johnny Magory,

His sister Lily-May and their trusty dog Ruairi.

The clever two are three and seven years old,

They're **usually** good

but they're

sometimes

bold!

On most summer evenings, the family take a walk,

Down by the old canal where they sing and talk.

The **midges** are out in force taking **bites** from everyone,

But nobody really minds because they're having so much fun!

They see their Grandad Paddy making flowerpots for his boat.

Johnny and Lily-May run over and snuggle into his old coat.

"Sure look it," Paddy says,

Will you join me on a cruise?
There's a **problem** with a lock gate
and there's no time to lose!

Johnny loves his Grandad's barge where he can wander and roam,

There's a kitchen, a bathroom and two bedrooms in the **floating** home.

Mammy puts on the **life jackets**, as Paddy cranks the engine to life.

The kids love the orange life vests, with the white reflective stripe.

The canals were made years ago for barges,

Paddy shouts.

For a **path through Ireland,**
so merchants could get about.
Their faithful **horses** would pull
the barges full of cargo along.
The men would **laugh** and **talk**
and **sing** a boatman's song.

OLAGH

Johnny **loves** listening to Paddy as he stands and helps him steer,
And he learns more about Ireland's canals every single year!

Johnny spots **Mr Otter** waving like mad from the bank,
He somersaults into the water from the diving plank!

We're going to have a race, will you and Ruairi join in?

That'll be grand, says Johnny. Sure we might even win!

Ahoy, there!

shouts Paddy, as they approach the broken lock.

He ties up "Coolagh" the barge on the **black** wooden block.

Mammy and Lily-May pick **blackberries**

as the men start fixing the gate.

Daddy **warns** Johnny and Ruairi,

Don't go **wandering** and come back late.

I promise I'll be back on time,

Johnny says to his **smiling** dad.

He never **means** to get in trouble or to make his parents mad!

Mr Otter leads them down the steep bank to a **special** place,

To a stream that runs under the canal, to have a **water race**.

The Duck family are there with Heron and lots of frogs.

Dusty the old barge horse shows

them a raft made of logs.

Dusty takes the thick rope,
one of a mighty Irish team,
He's going to pull Johnny and
Ruairi down the shallow stream.

Mr Otter has a **fine boat**, made from moss and twigs and rope,

The ducks' boat is made of lily-pads and is the **fastest** they hope!

Heron is at the starting line, getting them ready to **begin**.

Ms Swan is at the **finish line**,

to see who will win.

Heron flaps his wings,

The race **begins** with

everybody lined up in a row.

On your marks,
get set,
GO!

Mrs Pike joins in too, so the stream is pretty **tight**,

But **steady** Dusty pulls them along, a job he's done all his life.

Mr Otter's boat gets tangled up in the thick bullrush,

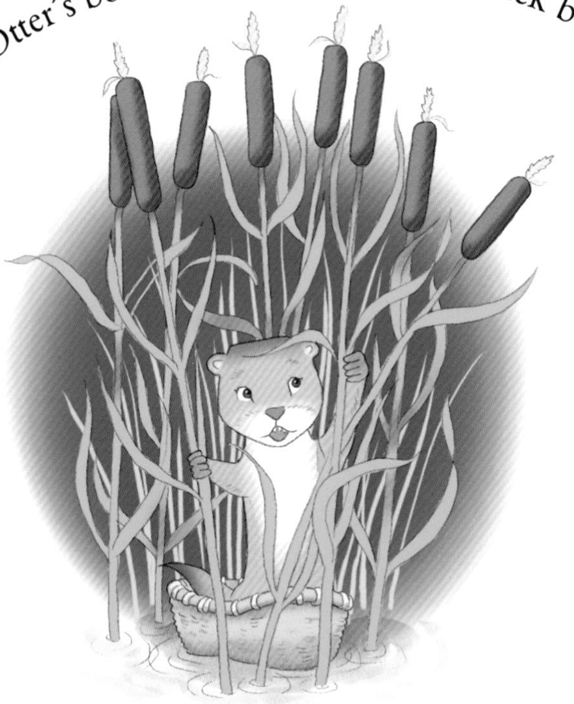

The ducks are so busy **quacking** they sail into a bush!

Mr Trout and Mrs Pike swim so **fast** they are nearly there,

But they see a swarm of flies and start **feasting** elsewhere!

Faithful Dusty keeps on going, one slow step at a time,

Johnny shouts **"Hooray"**, as they pass the finish line!

Ms Swan says,

You're the winners, there's no shadow of a doubt!

Johnny rubs the horse's ears and laughs,

We're happy out!

Ruairi hears Mammy shouting, so they have to make a run,

Back up to the canal to tell Lily-May about all the **fun!**

Mammy is **fierce angry** as Johnny appears from up the slope,

You put the heart crossways on me!

she says, untying the rope.

"I'm really sorry," says Johnny, "I didn't mean to be late."

"Ah don't worry," says Paddy, "we've just finished the gate."

Everyone gets back on the barge and Johnny sits beside Lily-May,

And as Mammy gets berries and ice-cream, he tells her about his day.

Lily-May hears about the race and all his exciting friends,

He fills her in on Dusty, Heron, Ms Swan and how it ends.

Lily-May **can't wait** until she's old enough to go too,

I'm dying to join Johnny and Ruairi on the adventures they do!

Whist, macushla,

Mammy says to her small daughter.

You'll have **many** more years to enjoy life on the water!

When they get home, they brush their teeth and climb into their beds,

And dreams of Ireland's magical waterways fill their tired heads.

Johnny can't help wondering what his next adventure will be,

And he promises Lily-May,

I'll bring you along with me!

Can you name Johnny Magory's friends?

Why not have your own adventure?

"Johnny Magory and the Wild Water Race" was inspired by the river Slate that flows under the Grand Canal near Lowtown Marina in county Kildare, Ireland.

Why not pack a picnic and take a little explorer on an adventure to try and catch a glimpse of Mr Otter, Heron and all their friends?